INTRODUCING
The Fenderbenders

NEW
YORK
Florida
PARTY
ANIMAL
Dad
Mom
Chrystal
Todd
Maniac

See if you can find America's zaniest family in...

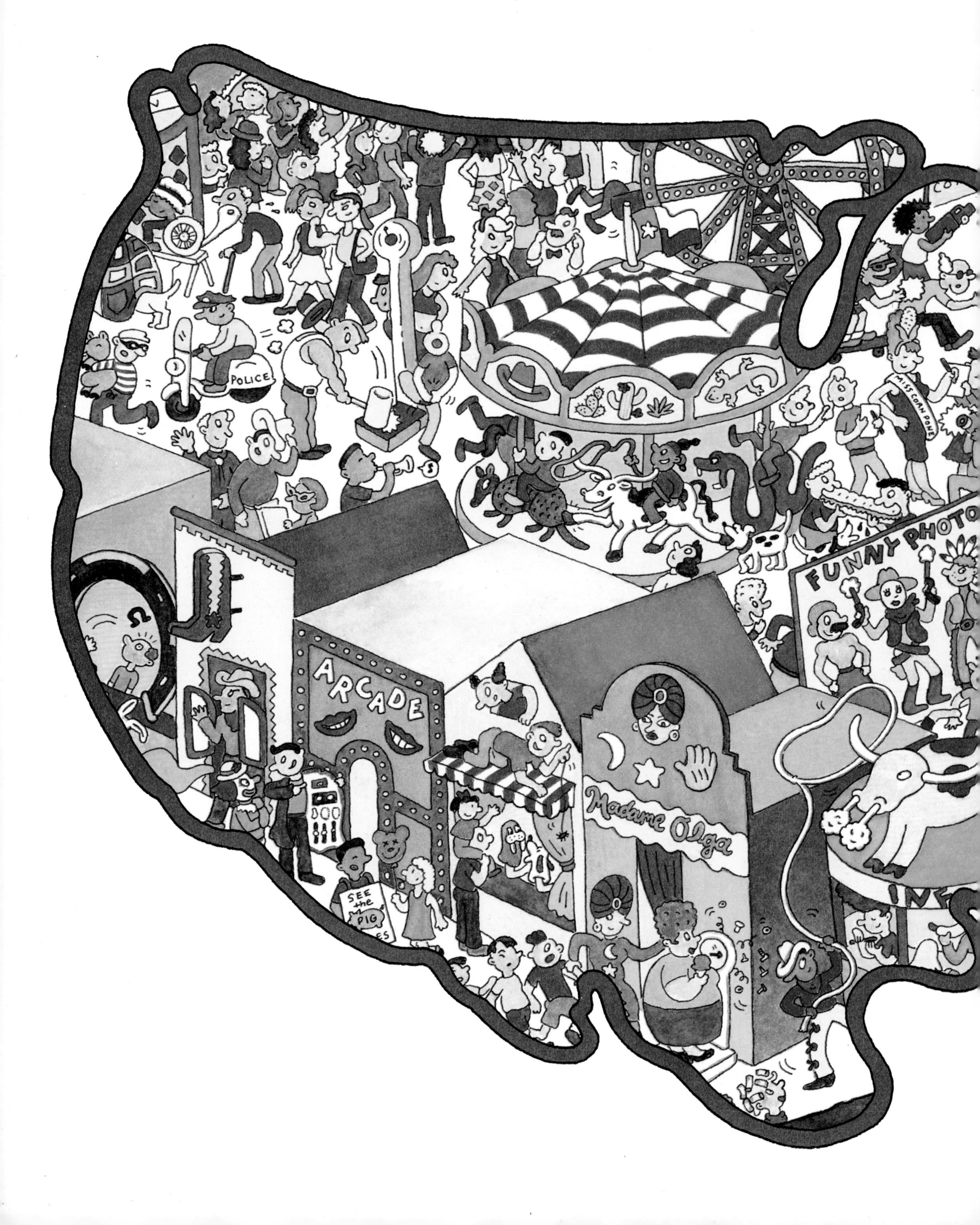

The Fenderbenders Get Lost in America

SCHOLASTIC INC.
New York Toronto London Auckland Sydney

To Arthur and Leonie

ISBN 0-590-44845-5

12 11 10 9 8 7 6 5 4 3 2 1   1 2 3 4 5 6/9

Printed in the U.S.A.   08

First Scholastic printing, August 1991

Dear Diary,
I can't believe our family is driving cross-country after spending our whole lives in Festerville! All us Fenderbenders are going - Mom, Dad, my obnoxious brother Todd, even our dog, Maniac. This would be the perfect family vacation - if only my family wasn't with me.
Love,
Chrystal
Chrystal's Travel Diary
KEEP OUT
Todd That Means You!
Dear Diary,
So we're going on this vacation, right? Finally I get to check out New York, D.C., Miami Beach, Texas, Mt. Rushmore, and L.A. Too bad my obnoxious sister is going too. Let's get one thing straight. Mom is making me keep this diary, but I'm still a radical dude.
Later,
Todd
AGAINST MY WILL
TODD'S DIARY
UNDER PROTEST
NO WAY JOSÉ
BEWARE! MUTANT RADIATION RAYS INSIDE

Dear Diary,
New York City is out of control. Mom better watch out—in her yellow dress, she looks like a taxi. What if someone tries to Flag her down?
That would be so righteous!
Later,
Todd
GOOD FOR ONE FARE
EMPIRE STATE BUILDING
ADMIT ONE
SHECKY TAUBMAN JEWELER TO THE STARS
DR LOTTA PAYNE D.D.S.
FUNNY NOSES SOLD HERE
FRUITS & VEGETABLES
PIZZA city
Madame Zoe
PALM READER
Curl up & Dye
HAIR SALON
BAGELMOBILE
JACOBS BAGELS BROS.
SESAME
"ANY FISH YOU WISH"
AL
DANGER
GIRLY
TRASH
NEW YORK MAP

Delici
Coff
BIG
PAGODA
RESTAURANT
BIJOU
Bijou
KING KONG
CIGARS
CANDY
Coca-Cola
ICE CREAM
SODA
"WE'RE OPEN 'TILL WE'RE CLOSED"
BIG
PAGODA
ROYAL
TV 3
SUBWAY
NYFD
TAXI
STATUE OF LIBERTY GUIDE
TOYS 4 SALE

See if *you* can find the Fenderbenders in New York City, not to mention the

- [ ] Chef of hot dogs
- [ ] Apple core
- [ ] Goofy fire fighter
- [ ] Lovesick mice
- [ ] Statue of Liberty
- [ ] Megaphone man
- [ ] King Kong
- [ ] Exploding fire hydrant
- [ ] Giant doggie bag
- [ ] Watch seller
- [ ] Sesame-seed tire
- [ ] Palm tree rooftop
- [ ] Pizza tosser
- [ ] Poodle lady
- [ ] Flower seller
- [ ] Guitar serenader
- [ ] Mona Lisa
- [ ] Musical police officer
- [ ] Trash thrower
- [ ] Big Pagoda cat
- [ ] Gun-toting policeman
- [ ] Alligator windup toy
- [ ] Cement lady
- [ ] Camera-mad tourists
- [ ] Chopstick holder
- [ ] Seeing blind man
- [ ] Pizza-catching dog
- [ ] Bubble-blowing fire fighter
- [ ] Flying teeth
- [ ] Moving TV set
- [ ] Sign painter
- [ ] Man with fish in his mouth
- [ ] Woman sporting a beehive-do
- [ ] Flamingo
- [ ] Subway motorist

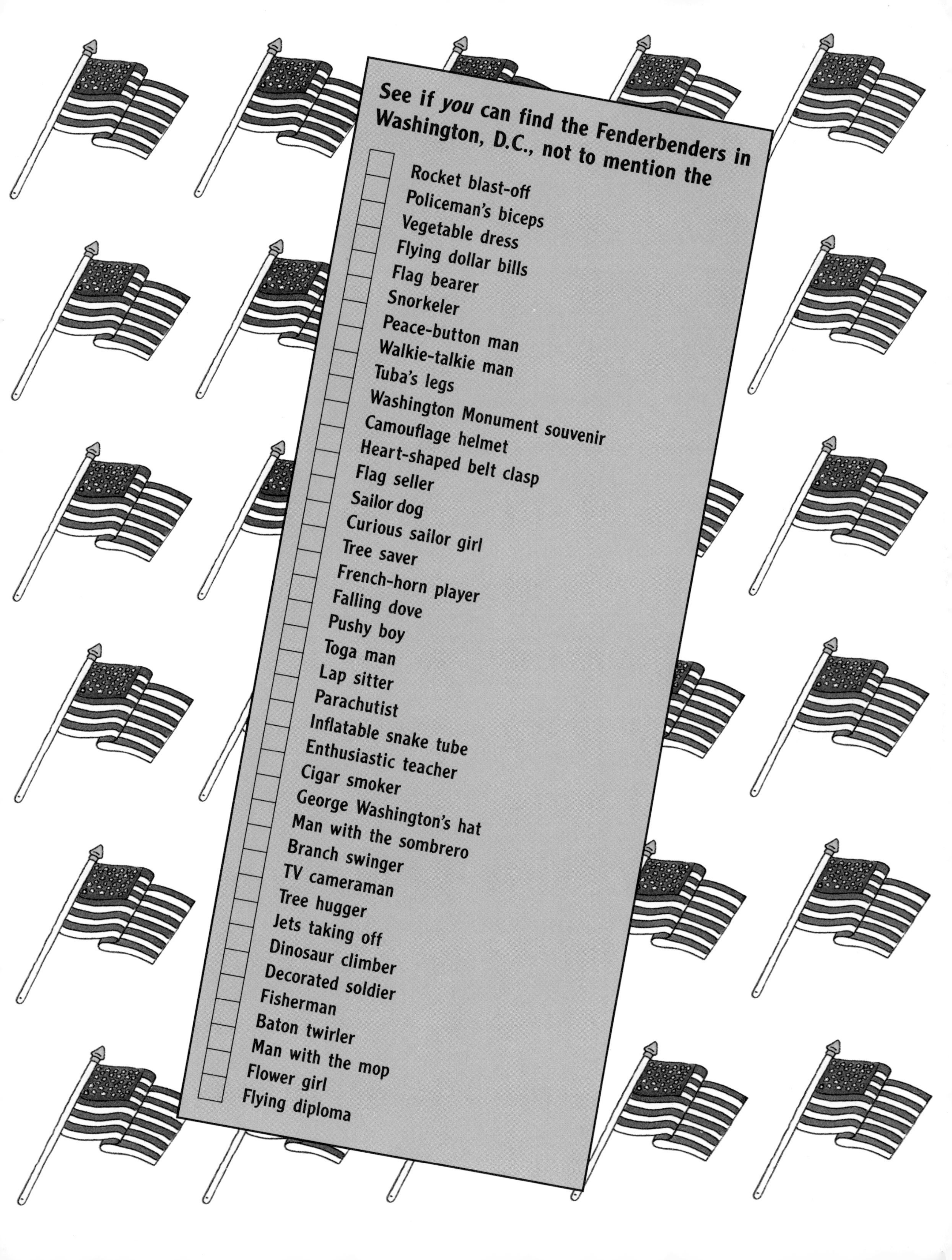
See if *you* can find the Fenderbenders in Washington, D.C., not to mention the
Rocket blast-off
Policeman's biceps
Vegetable dress
Flying dollar bills
Flag bearer
Snorkeler
Peace-button man
Walkie-talkie man
Tuba's legs
Washington Monument souvenir
Camouflage helmet
Heart-shaped belt clasp
Flag seller
Sailor dog
Curious sailor girl
Tree saver
French-horn player
Falling dove
Pushy boy
Toga man
Lap sitter
Parachutist
Inflatable snake tube
Enthusiastic teacher
Cigar smoker
George Washington's hat
Man with the sombrero
Branch swinger
TV cameraman
Tree hugger
Jets taking off
Dinosaur climber
Decorated soldier
Fisherman
Baton twirler
Man with the mop
Flower girl
Flying diploma

Dear Diary,
This place has monuments a-go-go! Dad thinks the White House would look better with pink flamingos on the lawn. Get real!
Todd, if you're reading this, you're dead meat.
Love,
Chrystal
Capitol
SOUVENIRS
D.C.
US MAIL
BUREAU OF ENGRAVING & PRINTING
SOLAR POWER NOW
SAVE the TREES
STOP OIL SPILLS
POLICE

STOP AIR POLLUTION
USA
Dinosaur Exhibit
TIONAL AIR &
ACE MUSEUM
POTOMAC CLEANERS "NO JOB TOO MONUMENTAL"
D.C.
Sit on Lincoln's Lap 25¢
RECYCLE
SAVE $ SHOP AT DISCOUNT DAN'S
SAVE the WHALES
TV 10
ANIMAL RIGHTS
RUDE DUDE

Dear Diary,
Miami Beach.
Pretty excellent.
So many boogie boards, so little time.
But I can't figure this out. Why do people wear fur coats to the beach?
Chrystal, I wouldn't read your stupid diary if you paid me.
Later-much,
Todd
MOST DEF BOOGIE BOARD
Fish 'n Tell Motel
PINK FLAMIN
MUSCLE MANIA
Ruth
EAT Florida ORANGES
Miami
JUDGE
SAND CASTLE CONTEST

PINK
FLAMINGO
HOTEL
MOTEL
SEAWEED
Dolph-Inn
ORANGE-O-RAMA
DRINK
TEENY BIKINI CONTEST
SILLY SHADES
BIG FISH CONTEST
JAWS

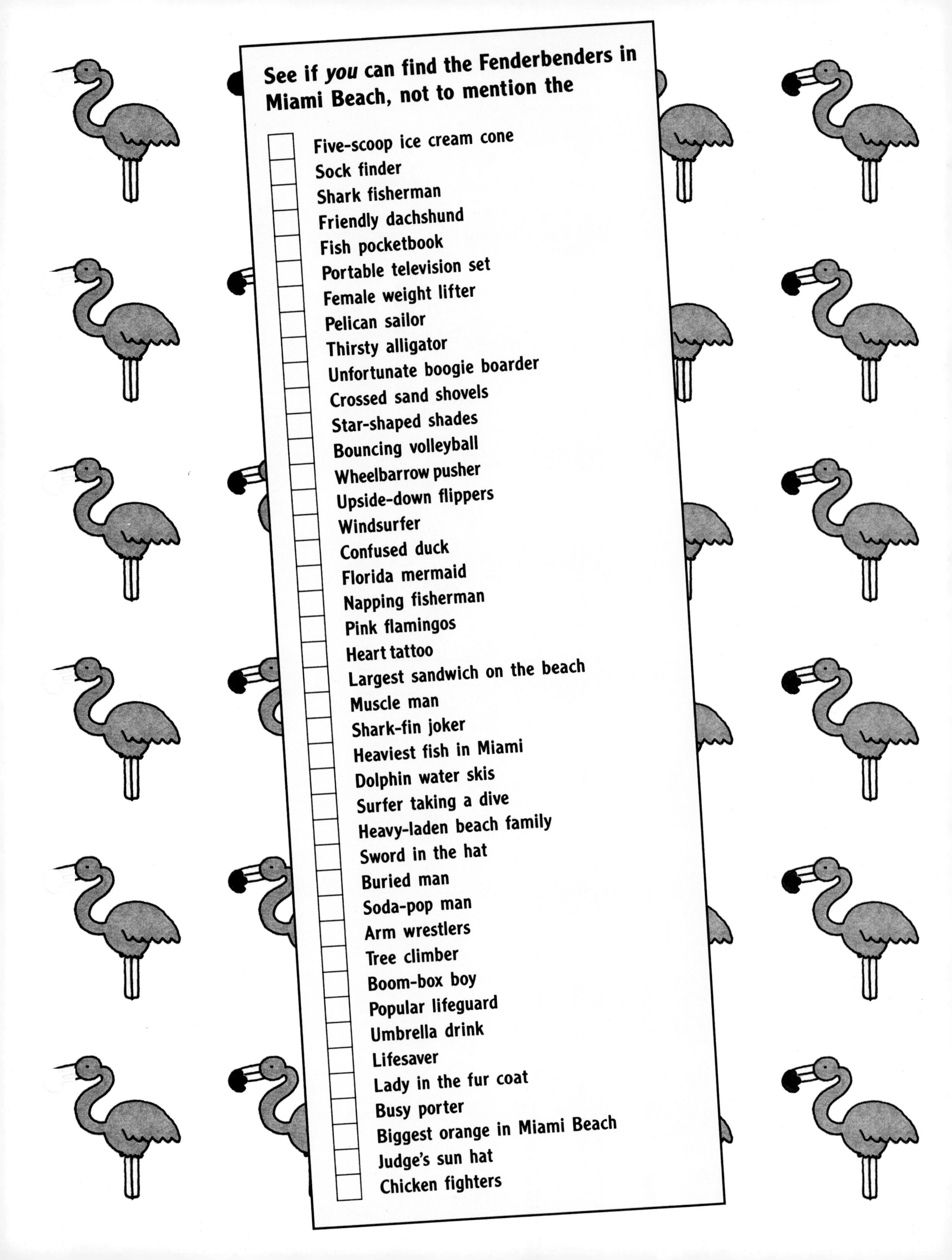

See if *you* can find the Fenderbenders in Miami Beach, not to mention the
Five-scoop ice cream cone
Sock finder
Shark fisherman
Friendly dachshund
Fish pocketbook
Portable television set
Female weight lifter
Pelican sailor
Thirsty alligator
Unfortunate boogie boarder
Crossed sand shovels
Star-shaped shades
Bouncing volleyball
Wheelbarrow pusher
Upside-down flippers
Windsurfer
Confused duck
Florida mermaid
Napping fisherman
Pink flamingos
Heart tattoo
Largest sandwich on the beach
Muscle man
Shark-fin joker
Heaviest fish in Miami
Dolphin water skis
Surfer taking a dive
Heavy-laden beach family
Sword in the hat
Buried man
Soda-pop man
Arm wrestlers
Tree climber
Boom-box boy
Popular lifeguard
Umbrella drink
Lifesaver
Lady in the fur coat
Busy porter
Biggest orange in Miami Beach
Judge's sun hat
Chicken fighters

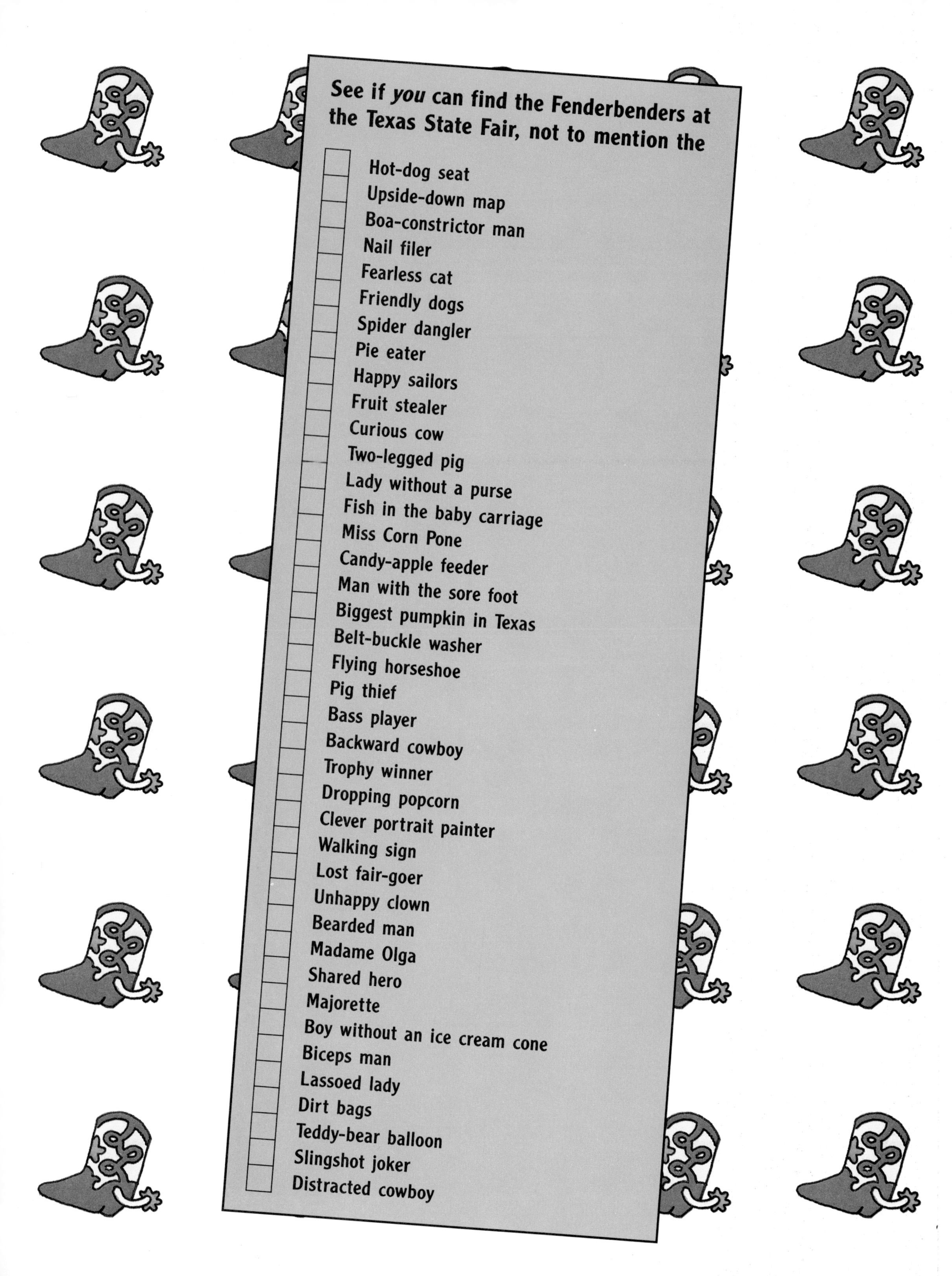
See if *you* can find the Fenderbenders at the Texas State Fair, not to mention the
Hot-dog seat
Upside-down map
Boa-constrictor man
Nail filer
Fearless cat
Friendly dogs
Spider dangler
Pie eater
Happy sailors
Fruit stealer
Curious cow
Two-legged pig
Lady without a purse
Fish in the baby carriage
Miss Corn Pone
Candy-apple feeder
Man with the sore foot
Biggest pumpkin in Texas
Belt-buckle washer
Flying horseshoe
Pig thief
Bass player
Backward cowboy
Trophy winner
Dropping popcorn
Clever portrait painter
Walking sign
Lost fair-goer
Unhappy clown
Bearded man
Madame Olga
Shared hero
Majorette
Boy without an ice cream cone
Biceps man
Lassoed lady
Dirt bags
Teddy-bear balloon
Slingshot joker
Distracted cowboy

Dear Diary,
Live cowboys, awesome. At the rodeo, one of them slipped and lassoed Mom's wig. Bummer! Time to get my prize for being a party animal–
Be cool,
Todd
Tunnel of Love
The Dirt Bags
Craft
EXHIBITION
POLICE
TEXAS
BIGGEST PUMPKIN IN TEXAS
EAT TEXAS HOT PEPPERS
ARCADE
SEE the PIG RACES
I'M WITH STUPID
MOM
WORLD'S BIGGEST MAN
Wild FIVE LEGGED BULL
SEE THE Doll Lady
oscar and his FABULOUS PERFORMING FLEAS
MAP

DANGER
CONSTRUCTION
RODEO
MISS CORN PONE
FUNNY PHOTOS
me Olga
INFORMATIO
Texas State Fair

Dear Diary,
Check out Mt. Rushmore! The Faces are so big our whole family could fit on Lincoln's left earlobe. Or on Washington's eyebrow. No sweat. Todd belongs up Jefferson's nose.
Love,
Chrystal
MT RUSHMORE
DRY GULCH GOLD MINE
U-PAN-IT
PAN YOUR OWN GOLD
COWBOYS
COWGIRLS
ZOO
Old West
MUSEUM
ROYAL ORDER OF THE BUFFALO
Your Photo at Mt. Rushmore!
JACK-E-LOPE RIDES 25¢

MAINTENANCE
EAT AT BOB'S
CHEEPEE TEEPEE
HOW CANOE RESIST?
TRAM RIDES
out POINT
Buffalo
BOBS
CHEEPEE TEEPEE
CALAMITY JANE R.I.P.
COLORADO CHARLIE
WILD BILL HICKOCK
TRAIL
Buffalo Bob's
SOUVENIRS
WHAT ME WORRY
CHEEPEE TEEPEE
EAT AT Buffalo Bob's
Mt Rushmore
Florida

See if *you* can find the Fenderbenders in Mount Rushmore, not to mention the

- [ ] Scoutmaster
- [ ] Rabbit chaser
- [ ] Five-burger eater
- [ ] Trumpet player
- [ ] Dog biter
- [ ] Calamity Jane's final resting place
- [ ] Dangling boy
- [ ] Romantic moose
- [ ] Four-legged chair-lift rider
- [ ] Runaway car
- [ ] Flying cowboy hat
- [ ] First family
- [ ] Sheriff
- [ ] Cotton swab
- [ ] Rattlesnake
- [ ] Toy plane
- [ ] Duck with a cold neck
- [ ] Lollipop
- [ ] Coonskin cap
- [ ] Crawler
- [ ] Braid puller
- [ ] Frightened man
- [ ] Glass dropper
- [ ] Nail in the bun
- [ ] Ménage à trois
- [ ] Garden shears
- [ ] Parachutist
- [ ] Totem pole
- [ ] Mountain climber
- [ ] Bow and arrow
- [ ] Pickpocket
- [ ] Gold panners
- [ ] Thirsty hardhat digger
- [ ] Bumpers
- [ ] Tree climber
- [ ] Sleepy cowboy
- [ ] Jack-o-lope
- [ ] Beanie cap

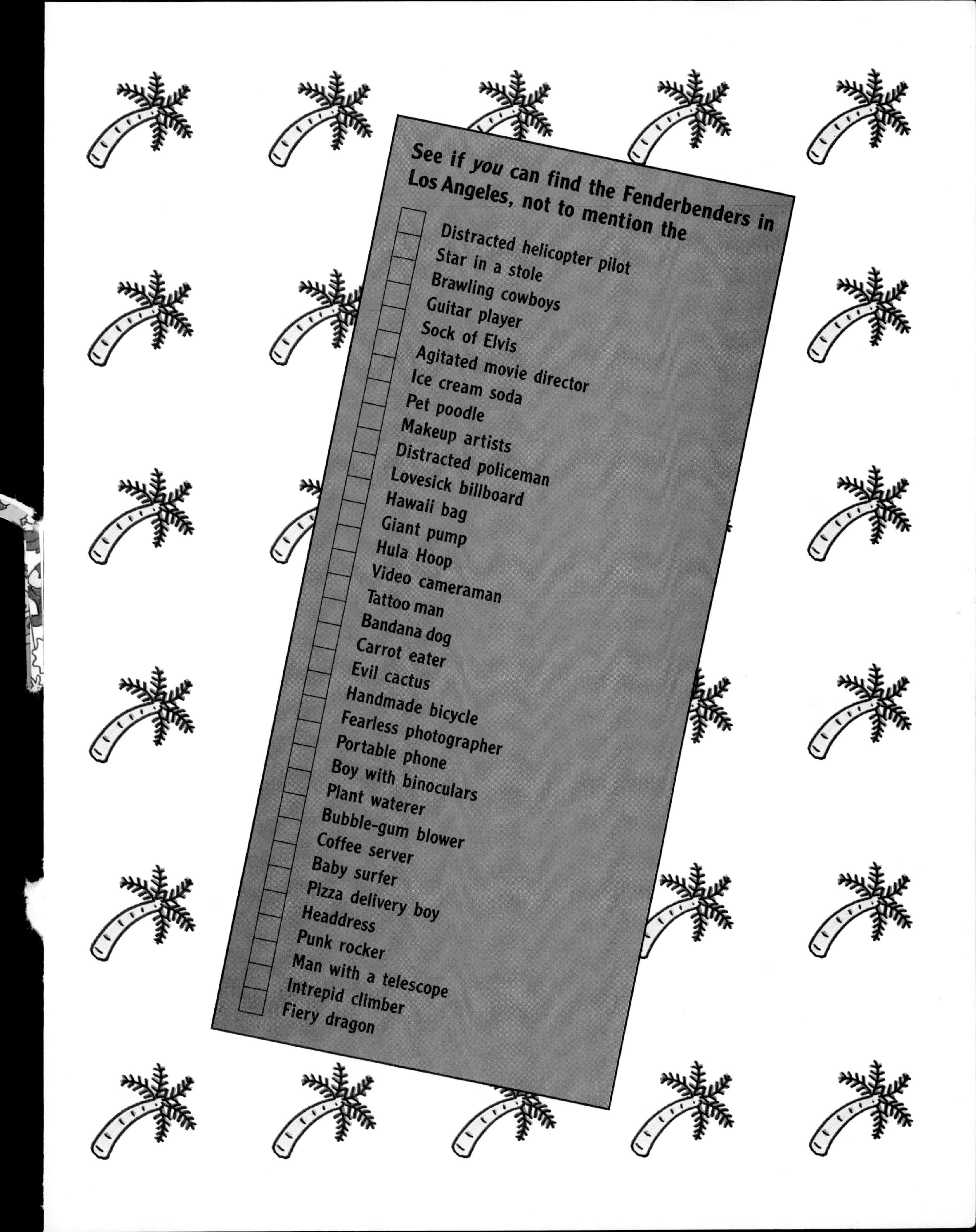
See if *you* can find the Fenderbenders in Los Angeles, not to mention the
Distracted helicopter pilot
Star in a stole
Brawling cowboys
Guitar player
Sock of Elvis
Agitated movie director
Ice cream soda
Pet poodle
Makeup artists
Distracted policeman
Lovesick billboard
Hawaii bag
Giant pump
Hula Hoop
Video cameraman
Tattoo man
Bandana dog
Carrot eater
Evil cactus
Handmade bicycle
Fearless photographer
Portable phone
Boy with binoculars
Plant waterer
Bubble-gum blower
Coffee server
Baby surfer
Pizza delivery boy
Headdress
Punk rocker
Man with a telescope
Intrepid climber
Fiery dragon

Dear Diary,
Like I can't believe we're finally in Hollywood. Every guy here is a major hunkasaurus. I just know one of them will find me and make me a star. Like if it doesn't happen soon, I'll have to go back to Festerville.
Kiss-Kiss,
Chrystal
HOLLYWOO
GUITAR CITY
CRAZY TACO
STAR DINER EAT
DINER
Radical RECORDS
MANN'S
CHINESE
GUITAR City
WAX M
TOUR-HOMES STARS
ELVIS
PIZZA

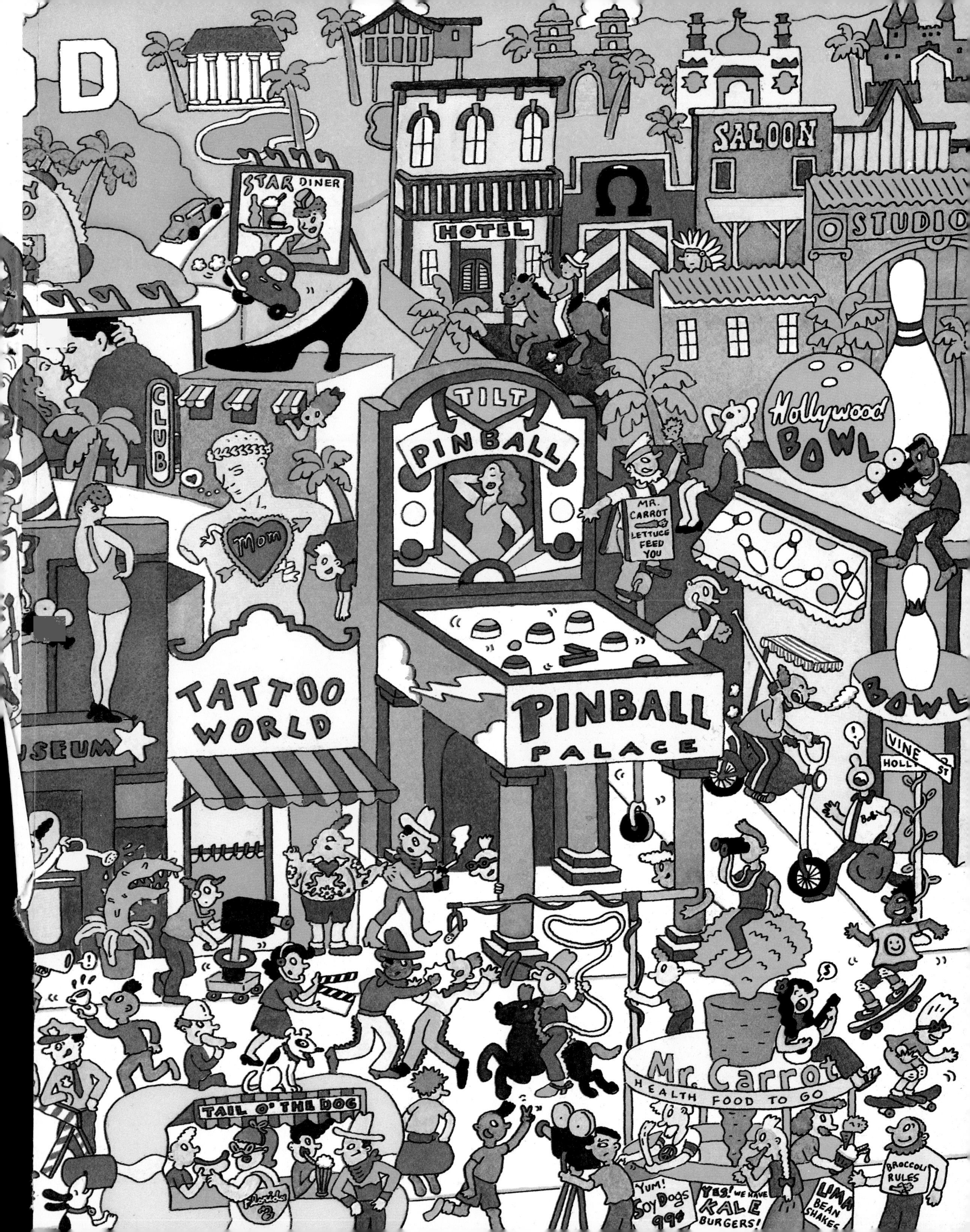

STAR DINER
HOTEL
SALOON
STUDIO
CLUB
TILT
PINBALL
Hollywood BOWL
MR. CARROT LETTUCE FEED YOU
Mom
TATTOO WORLD
PINBALL PALACE
BOWL
VINE ST
Bob
Mr. Carrot
HEALTH FOOD TO GO
TAIL O' THE DOG
YUM! SoyDogs 99¢
YES! WE HAVE KALE BURGERS!
LIMA BEAN SHAKES
BROCCOLI RULES

Dear Diary,

What a crazy trip this was! Mom ate, Dad drove, Maniac drooled, Todd played air guitar.... Maybe if we're really really good next year, we won't have to go on another one!

Love,
Chrystal

Chrystal's Travel Diary

KEEP OUT

Todd That Means You!

Dear Diary,

I thought this trip would never end! I had a pretty excellent time though considering who was with me. I wasn't bored at all, until I started reading Chrystal's diary.

I'm outta here,
Todd

P.S. I wonder where our next vacation will be....

AGAINST MY WILL

TODD'S DIARY

UNDER PROTEST

NO WAY JOSÉ

BEWARE! MUTANT RADIATION RAYS INSIDE